Fucking Colour Test Page!

Bitch Bitch Bitch

Shit Shit Shit

Fuck Fuck Fuck

Ass Ass Ass

Just have fun Bitches!

Cheers... Fuck Yes!

Cheers

Cheers

Cheers... Fuck Yes!

Cheers... Fuck Yes!

Are you happy now? Cheers

4

Energy Level ①②③④⑤

Date:

I Believe... I Got this Notes!

1.

2.

3.

4.

5.

6.

5:00 am	
6:00 am	
7:00 am	
8:00 am	
9:00 am	
10.00 am	
11:00 am	
12:00 pm	
1:00 pm	
2:00 pm	
3:00 pm	
4:00 pm	
5:00 pm	
6:00 pm	
7:00 pm	
8:00 pm	
9:00 pm	
10:00 pm	
11:00 pm	
12:00 am	
1:00 am	

Be Yourself

Text Today

Email Today

Today's Bitch Meter

◯ Walk? ◯ Lazy? ◯ Zen?

Bitch Moody Happy

Energy Level ① ② ③ ④ ⑤

Fucking Amazing Day!

Fuck Me Meter

◯ Couch Potato? ◯ Chill Day? ◯ Fuck You Day?

Bitch Moody Happy

Energy Level ① ② ③ ④ ⑤

Fuck Me Day!

Let's Fucking Get Zen!

☐ Walk Today?

☐ Zen Now?

☐ Reading?

☐ Music?

Zen As Fuck!

Exercise?

Check a Box!

Relax and get Zen!

11

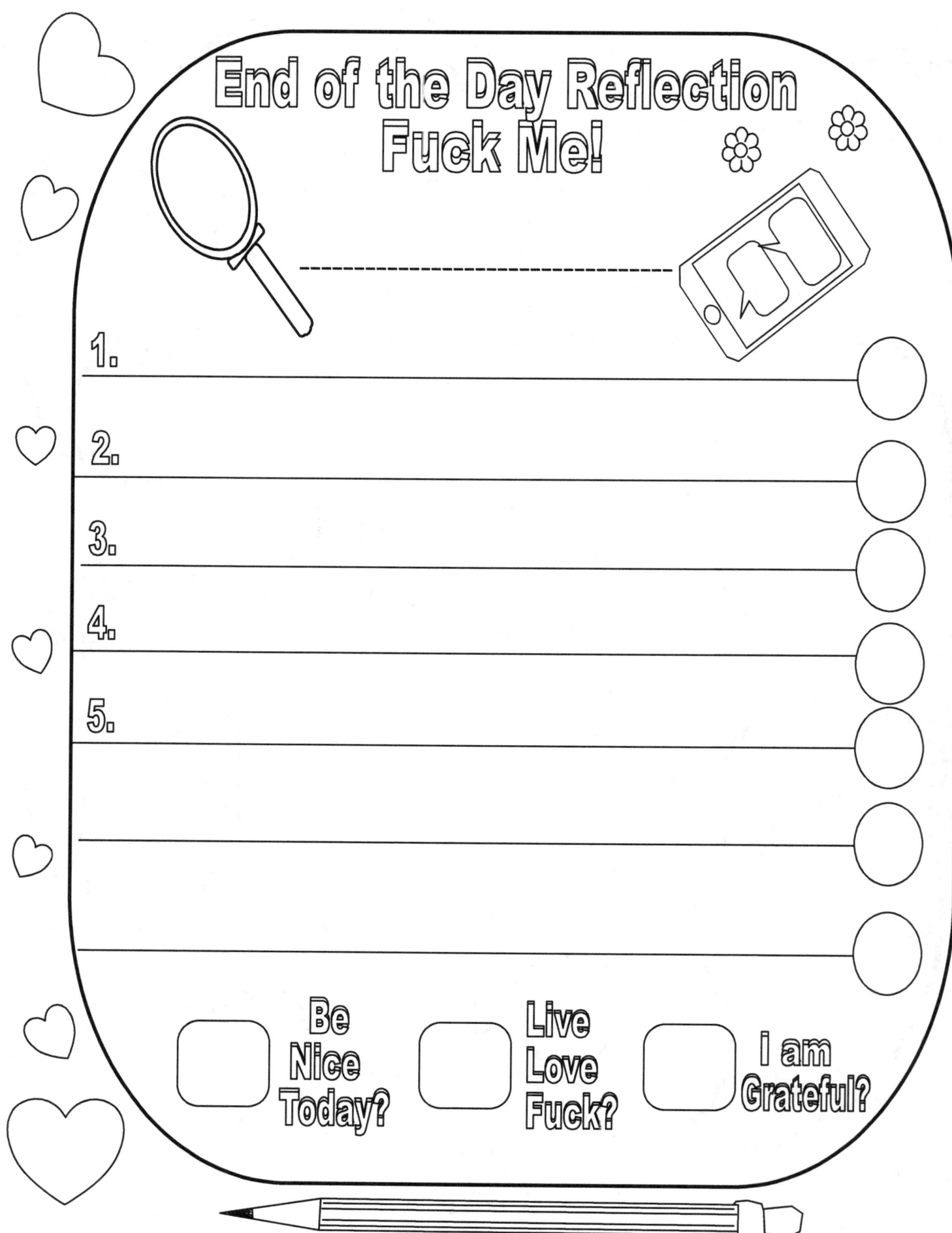

End of the Day Reflection
Fuck Me!

1.

2.

3.

4.

5.

☐ Be Nice Today?

☐ Live Love Fuck?

☐ I am Grateful?

My Bullshit Scribble!

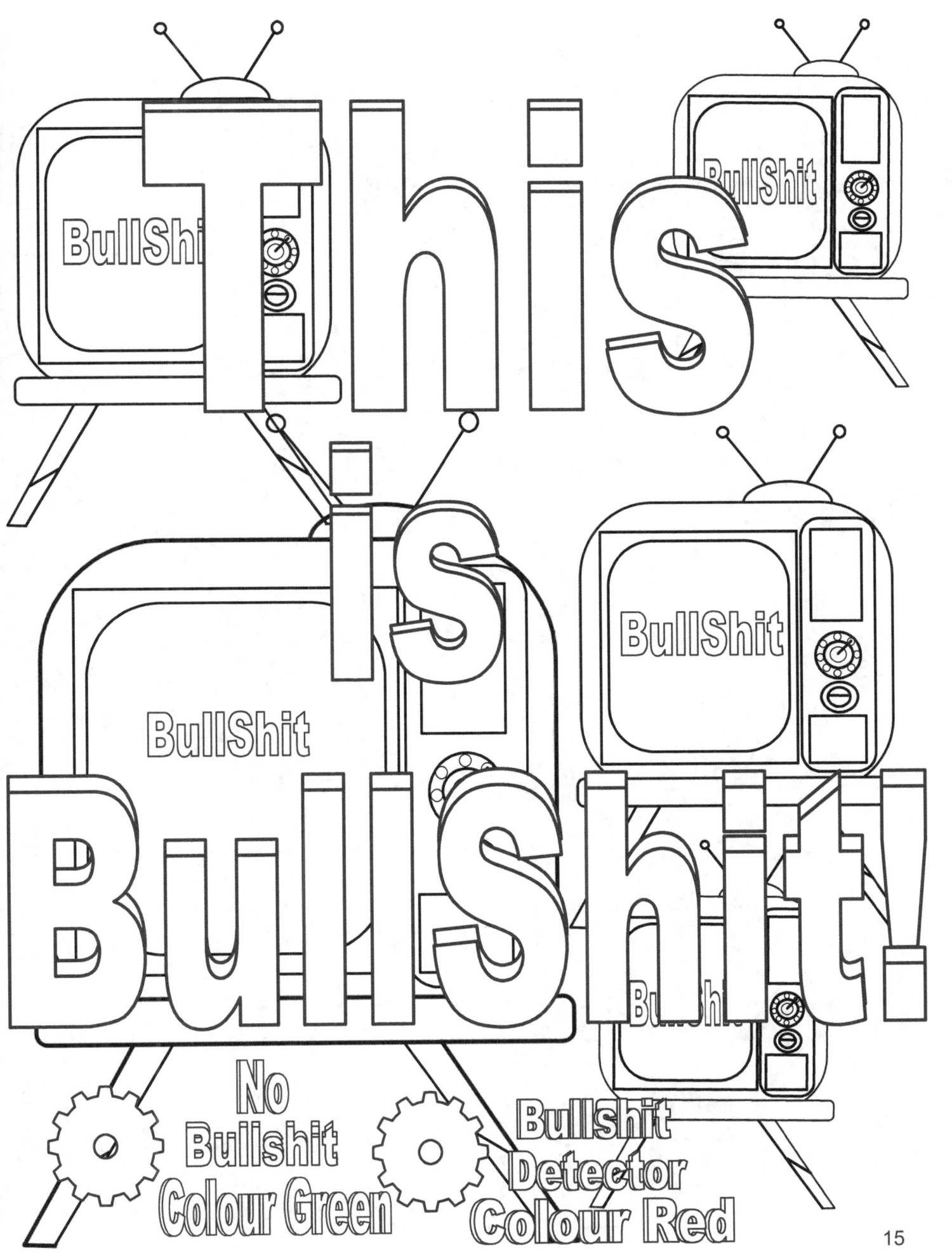

Zero Fucks Given!

Early to Bed?

Party Animal?

Fucking Tipsy?

Fucking Late for Work?

Coffee is My is My Super Power! Hell Yes!

is My Super Power! Hell Yes!

Shit....Can you Finish this?

Bitches...List your Fucking Favourite
Swearing Words?

1.

2.

3.

4.

23

My Besties... Asshole List

Love you Guys

My Besties... Bitches List

Love you Bitches

Bitch Scribble

24

1.

2.

3.

4.

5.

6.

What do you Kick Ass At?

Fill me in!

Empty Box

? ?

? ?

26

Fuck OFF OFF Fuck

Fuck OFF OFF

Fuck OFF OFF

Fuck OFF OFF

Fuck OFF Fuck OFF

Fuck OFF OFF

Fuck OFF OFF

Life is to Short....

Fucking

Make it Amazing

To Glamours to give a Shit!

I am a Fucking

Hell.....Can you Finish this?

Holy Shit...My Appointments for Today!

5:00 am		
6:00 am		
7:00 am		
8:00 am		
9:00 am		
10:00 am		
11:00 am		
12:00 pm		
1:00 pm		
2:00 pm		
3:00 pm		
4:00 pm		
5:00 pm		
6:00 pm		
7:00 pm		
8:00 pm		
9:00 pm		
10:00 pm		
11:00 pm		
12:00 am		
1:00 am		
2:00 am		

Late for Work?   Sick   Early As Shit   FML!

Forget Glass Slippers This Fucking Princess wears Motorcycle Boots!

Hello

Good Vibes Only

Hell..Colour this Button Red For Good Luck!

Colour the Button!

41

Hell... Be the Reason Someone Smiles Today

43

Love My Music
Song List

1. _____
2. _____
3. _____
4. _____
5. _____

minutes [ ]

My Social Life

[ ] Dancing

[ ] Party

Dam... Love My Exercise Time

Walk the Dog [ ]

Yoga [ ]

Jog [ ]

Shit...What makes me Happy!

DD   Pop   Chips

[ ] [ ] [ ] [ ] [ ]

Live Love Laugh

Swearing is a fucking sign of Intelligence

#Verbal Superiority

46

So Fucking true!!
IQ

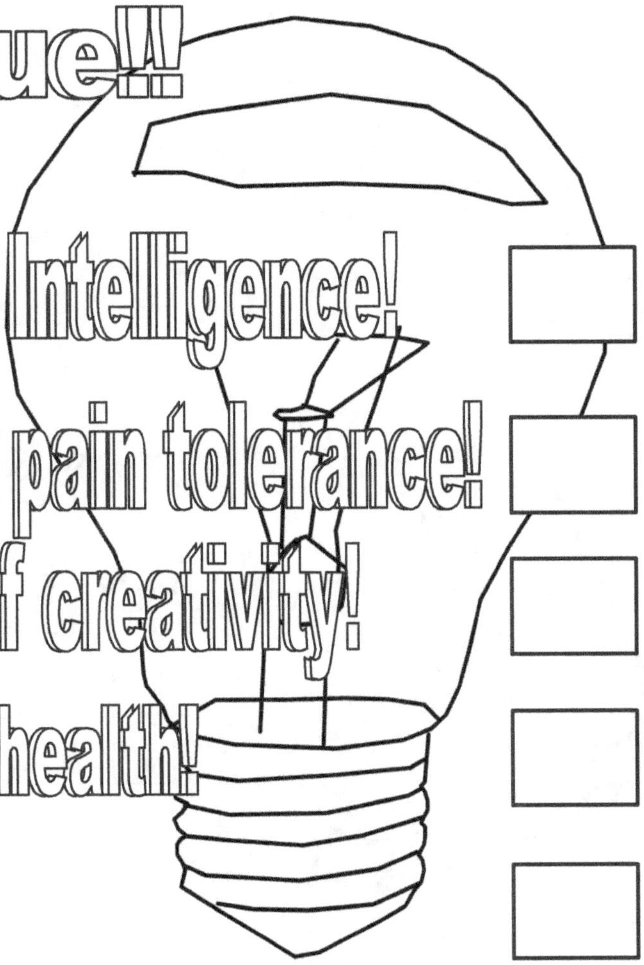

1. Swearing is a Sign of Intelligence! ☐

2. Profanity improves my pain tolerance! ☐

3. Swearing is a Sign of creativity! ☐

4. Swearing improves my health! ☐

5. _____ ☐

My Creativity Doodle

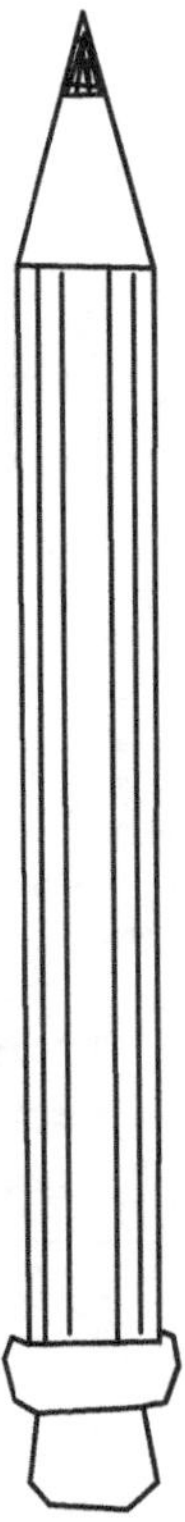

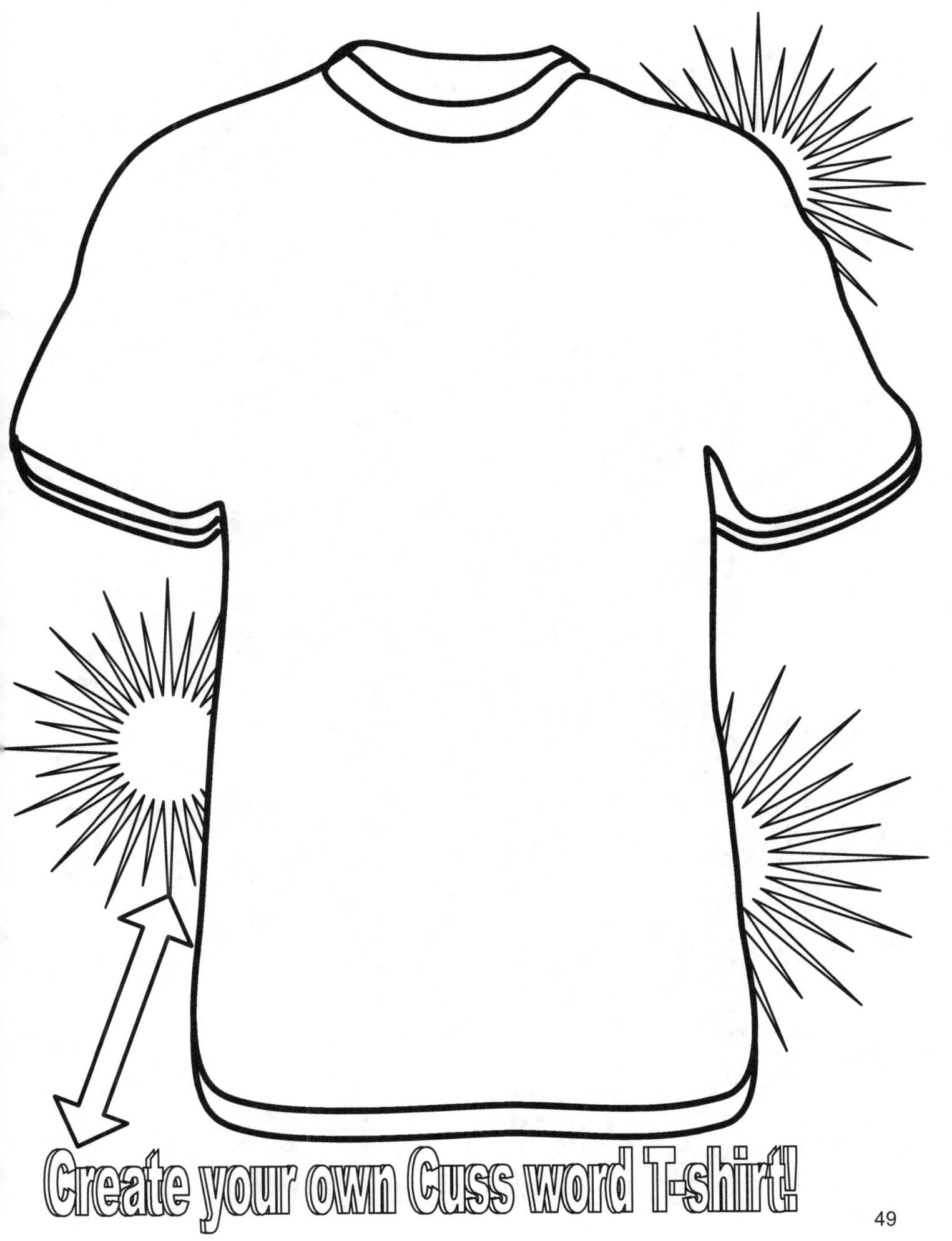

Create your own Cuss word T-shirt!

Shit for Brains...
Take only Memories
Leave No Trash!

Protect our Fucking Butterflies!

51

GUESS THESE SWEAR WORDS
(ABBREVIATIONS)

1. WTF?
2. WTAF?
3. WETF?
4. WTGDMF?
5. WTFO?

→ ANSWERS HERE!
BITCHES

1. _____
2. _____
3. _____
4. _____
5. _____

→ SCORE

HELL...DON'T PEEK AT THE ANSWERS YET!....
NO FUCKING PEEKING!

Stop

Stop

1. WHAT THE FUCK!
2. WHAT THE ACTUAL FUCK!
3. WHAT EVEN THE FUCK!
4. WHAT THE GODDAMN MOTHER FUCK!
5. WHAT THE FUCK OVER!

→CREATE YOUR OWN HERE!
BITCHES

1. _____

2. _____

3. _____

4. _____

DID YOU CHEAT?

5. _____

55

www.ingramcontent.com/pod-product-compliance
Lightning Source LLC
Chambersburg PA
CBHW080904120626
46555CB00008B/2957